I CAN READ IT ALL BY MYSELF

Beginner Books

I CAN READ IT ALL BY MYSELF

Beginner Books

SPOOKY RIDDLES

Marc Brown

HarperCollins *Children's Books*

Trademark of Random House Inc., William Collins & Co. Ltd., Authorised User

15 17 19 20 18 16 14

ISBN-10: 0-00-171423-6 (paperback)
ISBN-10: 0-00-171176-8 (hardback)
ISBN-13: 978-0-00-171423-6

A Beginner Book published by arrangement with
Random House Inc., New York, New York
First published in Great Britain in 1984

Visit our website at:
www.harpercollinschildrensbooks.co.uk

Printed and bound in Hong Kong

What does a mother ghost say
to her child when they get
into the car?

Why do skeletons hate winter?

The cold goes right through them.

Why was Dracula put in jail?

He tried to rob a blood bank.

What rides at the amusement park do ghosts like best?

The scary-go-round and
the roller ghoster.

What is the best way
to talk to a ghost?

Long distance.

What does a witch ask for when she arrives at a hotel?

Broom service.

Why do witches
fly on brooms?

Vacuum cleaners
are too heavy.

What do bats need after a shower?

A bat mat.

What time is it when a ghost comes to dinner?

Time to go!

What does a little witch
hope to get for her birthday?

A haunted doll's house.

What should you do
when you see a ghost?

Hope the ghost does not see you.

How does a witch tell the time?

With a witchwatch.

Why don't skeletons go to scary films?

They don't have the guts.

Why do vampires drink blood?

What do you call a mummy who eats biscuits in bed?

A crumby mummy.

Why do witches wear pointed hats?

To cover their pointed heads.

W hat yard will kids never play in?

A graveyard.

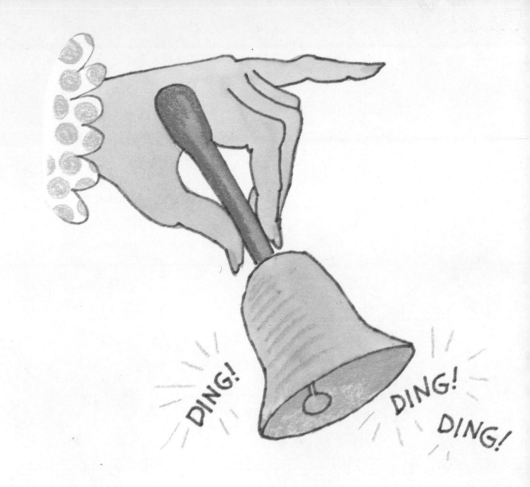

What do you get when you cross
a bell and a bat?

A dingbat.

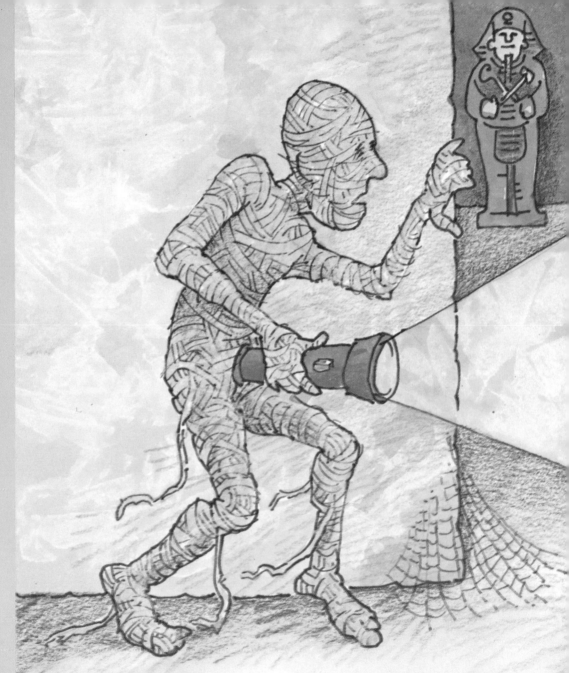

What did the detective mummy
say when he solved the case of
the missing cat?

"That about wraps it up."